THRASH   LASERMAN

To my dear children, Gillah & Mordechai, Dovid, Nechemiah, and Ezra:
You are each Superheroes, saving the world in your most super way! —S. B.

For my super-brother, Dahico! —E. K.

STERLING CHILDREN'S BOOKS
New York

An Imprint of Sterling Publishing Co., Inc.
1166 Avenue of the Americas
New York, NY 10036

ISBN 978-1-4549-1394-8

Distributed in Canada by Sterling Publishing Co., Inc.
c/o Canadian Manda Group, 664 Annette Street
Toronto, Ontario, Canada M6S 2C8
Distributed in the United Kingdom by GMC Distribution Services
Castle Place, 166 High Street, Lewes, East Sussex, England BN7 1XU
Distributed in Australia by NewSouth Books
45 Beach Street, Coogee, NSW 2034, Australia

For information about custom editions, special sales, and premium and corporate purchases,
please contact Sterling Special Sales at 800-805-5489 or specialsales@sterlingpublishing.com.

Manufactured in Canada

Lot #:
4 6 8 10 11 9 7 5 3
10/16

www.sterlingpublishing.com

The artwork for this book was created digitally.
Design by Andrea Miller and Irene Vandervoort

EVEN SUPERHEROES HAVE BAD DAYS

By **SHELLY BECKER** • Illustrated by **EDA KABAN**

STERLING CHILDREN'S BOOKS

New York

When superheroes don't get their way, when they're sad,
when they're mad, when they have a bad day . . .

. . . they could use super-powers to kick, punch, and pound.
They could shriek—they could screech with an ear-piercing sound.

They could crush wooden crates and bend metal gates.

They could throw trucks and buses across several states.

They could knock over buildings like towers of blocks
and crumble the streets into rubble and rocks.

They could use laser eyes to ignite forest fires,
or fling boomerangs to deflate the town's tires.

But upset superheroes have all sorts of choices. . . .

Instead of destruction and loud, livid voices
they burn angry steam off with speed-of-light hiking
or super-Xtreme outer space mountain biking.

They race to the rescue of people in need
and delight in the joy of a super-good deed.
They hatch super-plans to help banish world sadness,
building fabulous theme parks for giggles and gladness.

HOT DOGS & SAUSAGE

NEWS

They chase wanted bad guys with super-charged zing,
dragging hundreds to jail while police dance and sing.

They track down and tame super-menacing beasts
and transform pity parties to victory feasts.

But displeased superheroes who don't feel serene
could have super-temptation to cause a bad scene. . . .

They could blast icy blizzards on hot afternoons,
or walloping twisters and monster typhoons.

They could spin super-webs, super-far, super-sticky,
and tangle up towns with their silk—SUPER-ICKY!

They could rotate the planet
and mess up world time,

or sit back and relax while the world fills with crime.

When superheroes
don't get their way,
when they're sad,
when they're mad,
when they've had a bad day . . .

. . . they *could* super-rampage—they *could*, but they *don't*,
because *real* superheroes just *wouldn't*—they *won't*!

Instead they dig down to their super-best part,
the strong super-powers contained in their heart!

And using their talents as true heroes should,
they battle the urge to do harm (though they *could*).
They acknowledge their sorrow, their anger, their pain,
as they wait for their super-emotions to wane.

It's okay if they frown.

It's okay if they sigh.

It's even okay if they slump down and cry.

But then they get up and get on with their day . . .

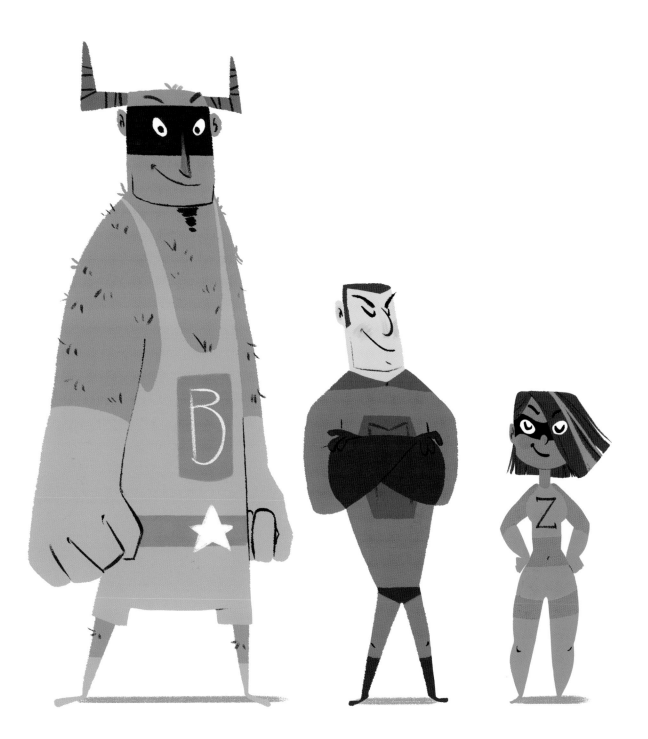

. . . saving the world in their most super way.

MAGNIFIQUE   SCREECHER